WITHDRAWN

RIVER FOREST PUBLIC LIBRARY
735 Lathrop Avenue
River Forest, Illinois 60305
708 / 366-5205

17

1/07

Science Matters
RAINBOWS

RIVER FOREST PUBLIC LIBRARY
735 LATHROP
RIVER FOREST, IL 60305

David Whitfield

WEIGL PUBLISHERS INC.

Published by Weigl Publishers Inc.
350 5th Avenue, Suite 3304, PMB 6G
New York, NY USA 10118-0069
Website: www.weigl.com

Copyright © 2007 WEIGL PUBLISHERS INC.
All rights reserved. No part of this publication may be reproduced, stored in a retrieval system, or transmitted in any form or by any means, electronic, mechanical, photocopying, recording, or otherwise, without the prior written permission of the publisher.

Library of Congress Cataloging-in-Publication Data

Whitfield, David.
  Rainbows / by David Whitfield.
      p. cm. -- (Science matters)
  Includes bibliographical references and index.
  ISBN 1-59036-414-7 (alk. paper) -- ISBN 1-59036-420-1 (pbk. : alk. paper)
  1. Meteorological optics--Juvenile literature. 2. Rainbow--Juvenile literature. I. Title. II. Series.
  QC975.3.W55 2007
  551.56'7--dc22

                            2005029921

Printed in China
1 2 3 4 5 6 7 8 9 10 09 08 07 06

Editor Frances Purslow
Design and Layout Terry Paulhus

Cover: Although rainbows occur when there is moisture in the air, they sometimes occur in dry areas following a storm.

Photograph Credits

University of Heidelberg, ESA: page 12T; **NASA,ESA, M. Robberto (Space Telescope Science Institute/ESA) and the Hubble Space Telescope Orion Treasury Project Team plus C.R. O'Dell (Rice University), and NASA**: pages 12 & 13 background; **NASA, ESA, J. Hester and A. Loll (Arizona State University)**: page 14L.

All of the Internet URLs given in the book were valid at the time of publication. However, due to the dynamic nature of the Internet, some addresses may have changed, or sites may have ceased to exist since publication. While the author and publisher regret any inconvenience this may cause readers, no responsibility for any such changes can be accepted by either the author or the publisher.

Every reasonable effort has been made to trace ownership and to obtain permission to reprint copyright material. The publishers would be pleased to have any errors or omissions brought to their attention so that they may be corrected in subsequent printings.

Contents

Studying Rainbows

Nature creates rainbows in the sky. Rainbows can be found almost anywhere in the world where there is rain. They appear after a rainstorm, when the Sun is shining.

Although there is no record of when the first rainbow was seen, humans have been interested in rainbows since early times. Ancient peoples thought rainbows appeared magically in the sky. They created **proverbs**, songs, and legends about them.

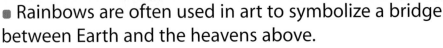
■ Rainbows are often used in art to symbolize a bridge between Earth and the heavens above.

Rainbow Facts

Did you know that rainbows are rarely seen at noon? The Sun must be behind the viewer for a rainbow to appear, and at noon the Sun is overhead. Read more interesting facts about rainbows below.

- Scientists believe that Titan, Saturn's moon, might have rainbows. Titan's air contains a type of gas that could create rainbows when the Sun shines.

- Large raindrops produce brighter red, orange, and yellow colors in the rainbow. Small raindrops produce brighter blues.

- When viewed from an airplane with the Sun behind it, a rainbow looks like a complete circle. The shadow of the plane will be in the middle.

Colors of the Rainbow

White light is made of many different colors. These colors are often seen in the sky during or after rain has fallen. Rainbow colors are created when sunlight shines on raindrops in the sky. Sunlight is made up of many colors of light people can see. It also contains colors people cannot see. When all colors are mixed together, sunlight looks white. But when sunlight is refracted, or bent, in a raindrop, it separates into seven colors. These are the colors in a rainbow.

■ Billions of raindrops are needed to make a rainbow.

Bending Light

Sunlight follows a straight line when it moves through the air. If it enters another substance, such as water or glass, it changes direction or bends. This bending is called refraction.

Light refraction can be studied using a prism. A prism is a triangle-shaped piece of glass or **acrylic**. When sunlight strikes the prism, the light does not shine through in a straight line. The light slows down and is bent as it enters the prism. Some colors of light bend more than others. Violet bends the most, and red bends the least.

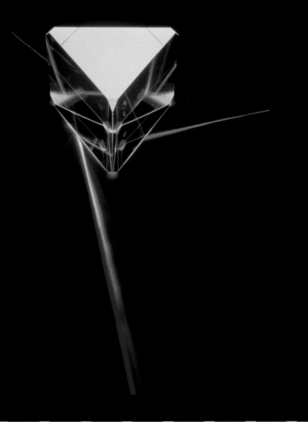

The bending separates the light into seven colors: red, orange, yellow, green, blue, indigo, and violet. When a single rainbow is seen, red is at the top and violet is at the bottom.

How Rainbows Form

Rainbows form when rain falls in one part of the sky while the Sun shines in another. Sunlight shining on raindrops in the sky creates a rainbow.

When sunlight strikes a raindrop, the raindrop acts like a prism. Each color of light bends or refracts at a different angle. It separates as it passes through the raindrop. After the light is bent inside the raindrop, it is reflected or bounced back toward the source of light. Then the light bends once more when it exits the raindrop.

■ Each raindrop reflects all the colors of the rainbow. However, the viewer sees only one color from each raindrop. The color depends on the raindrop's position in relation to the viewer.

Reflected Light

People seldom notice that the Sun is always behind them when they see a rainbow.

The center of a rainbow **arc** always appears in the sky opposite the Sun. This is because the raindrop reflects the sunlight back toward the Sun. In order for someone to see the rainbow, the Sun must be behind the viewer. The viewer's eyes see the colors as they reflect back from the raindrops.

Rainbow Variations

Sundogs and Halos

On some cold, clear days in winter, rainbow-like colors can be seen. When the Sun shines on ice crystals, a bright halo may appear around the Sun. Bright spots on either side of the halo are called sundogs. Most sundogs are white, but sometimes they are red on the inside and blue on the outside.

Low Rainbows

Rain is not necessary for rainbows to appear. However, there must be moisture in the air. Rainbows can be seen near waterfalls, as the Sun shines on the mist. Rainbows can also be seen in sprays made by garden hoses, lawn sprinklers, and fountains. Sometimes rainbows can be seen in spray from a boat.

Soap Bubbles and Oil Spills

Rainbow colors can be seen in soap bubbles or in oil spills on a wet road. They are not true rainbows, but can show the same colors.

Unlike rainbows, colors in bubbles and oil spills can shift and change. They swirl with the movement of the liquid they are in. When people look at this type of rainbow, the colors may change, depending on the point of view.

Sky Technology

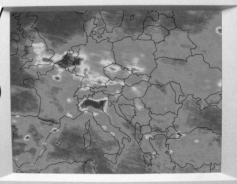

Geographic Information System (GIS)
Special computers called Geographic Information Systems (GIS) gather information about Earth. Scientists use GIS to map **air pollution** in cities and towns. Results are posted on the Internet so people can read about the types and amount of pollution where they live.

Telescopes
Telescopes help us see objects that are far away. Astronomers use them to observe space objects, such as stars, planets, and whole **galaxies**. Telescopes make distant objects appear closer by collecting light. Telescopes can collect more light than the human eye can.

Weather Satellite

Weather satellites are spacecraft that circle Earth. They provide a weather watch on the entire planet. Weather satellites take photographs of Earth's atmosphere. These help meteorologists predict storms and other weather patterns. These satellites also carry special instruments that record information on computers. They monitor events in the atmosphere, such as auroras, dust storms, pollution, and cloud systems.

Radar

Meteorologists gather huge amounts of information in order to predict the weather. **Radar** can tell them what is inside a cloud. This can be rain or hail. Radar can also track a storm that is coming. It helps meteorologists warn people if the storm is dangerous.

Double Rainbows

Sometimes nature creates two rainbows together. The rainbows are seen one above the other. When there are two rainbows, the lower one is called the primary rainbow. The higher one is a secondary rainbow.

Sunlight must be very strong to create two rainbows. The sunlight is reflected once in raindrops to make the primary rainbow. Then, if it is reflected again, it creates the secondary one. This rainbow is not as bright.

■ The colors of the secondary rainbow are reversed. Violet is at the top and red is at the bottom.

Bright Sky

The sky inside or below a rainbow is often brighter than the sky above or outside the rainbow. This is because light that is not reflected into the colors of the rainbow is scattered below it. Since this is white light, the sky looks brighter.

When there is a double rainbow in the sky, there is often a dark band between the two rainbows. This dark area is called Alexander's Dark Band. It is named after Alexander of Aphrodisias, a Greek **philosopher**. He first described it hundreds of years ago. This area is darker than the rest of the sky because the light reflected from the raindrops in this area is scattered above or below. It does not reach an observer's eyes.

Alexander's Dark Band

Lunar Rainbows

Sometimes a full moon can create a rainbow at night. This kind of rainbow is called a **lunar** rainbow. Lunar rainbows are rare.

Lunar rainbows are not as bright as rainbows that appear during the day. In fact, lunar rainbows are sometimes so pale that they appear as a white arc in the night sky. Like daytime rainbows, the source of light for lunar rainbows is sunlight. However, at night the sunlight bounces off the uneven surface of the moon and reflects to Earth. This results in a paler rainbow.

■ Rainbows that appear at sunset are often red.

Rainbow Folklore

Rainbows are featured in folklore around the world. One of the most popular stories is from Ireland. In Irish folklore, **leprechauns** are said to bury their pots of gold at the end of the rainbow.

In some African **myths**, the rainbow was a giant snake that hunted after a rainfall.

Some stories from Eastern Europe also feature the rainbow as a giant snake. The snake drank water from seas, lakes, and rivers, then sprinkled the water over the land as rain.

Long ago, people in Finland believed a rainbow was the bow used by the Thunder God to shoot arrows of lightning.

Rainbow Proverbs

For **centuries**, people have tried to **forecast** the weather. Long before weather bulletins on television or radio, people looked for weather clues in nature. They used proverbs to explain the weather. Some proverbs were based on the science of nature. This is an example of a weather proverb.

Rainbow to windward, foul fall the day,
Rainbow to leeward, rain runs away.

This proverb is based on the fact that if the wind is blowing from the direction of a rainbow, rain is coming toward you. If the wind is blowing toward a rainbow, then rain is moving away from you.

■ Here is a common weather proverb.
Rainbow at morning, shepherd take warning,
Rainbow at night, shepherd's delight.

A Life of Science

René Descartes

René Descartes was a French philosopher and **mathematician**. To learn about rainbows, he studied light striking and passing through a single large drop of water. Descartes made this large drop using a glass ball full of water. In 1637 he discovered that light was refracted in a raindrop, then reflected back out. Descartes found that a secondary rainbow is caused by light reflected twice in raindrops. He also realized that each color of white light exits a raindrop at a different angle, creating the colors of the rainbow.

Surfing Rainbow Science

How can I find more information about rainbows?
- Libraries have many interesting books about rainbows.
- Science centers and museums are great places to learn about rainbows.
- The Internet offers some great websites dedicated to rainbows.

Where can I find a good reference website to learn more about rainbows?
How Stuff Works Homepage
http://science.howstuffworks.com/
- Type "rainbow" into the search engine.

How can I find out more about rainbows?
Atmospheric Optics
www.atoptics.co.uk/
- Select "Rainbows."

Science in Action

Make Your Own Rainbow

Nature makes rainbows in the sky. On a sunny day, you can make one in your own yard.

You will need:

- a friend
- a garden hose
- a watering nozzle
- sunlight

Ask your friend to hold the hose and turn the nozzle to make a fine spray.

With your back to the Sun, look at the falling drops. Can you see a rainbow? If not, move your position until you see a rainbow reflected in the water drops.

Can you see all seven colors? Is there another rainbow above the first? Are the colors of the second rainbow the same?

Let your friend watch while you hold the hose and spray water in the air.

What Have You Learned?

1 What acts like a prism in the sky, bending light to create a rainbow?

2 In which season do sundogs appear?

3 What kind of light is needed to see a rainbow in the sky?

4 Who discovered that light was refracted in a raindrop and then reflected back out?

5 Which seven colors are in a rainbow?

6 Where must the Sun be for a person to see a rainbow?

7 Describe a secondary rainbow.

8 What is the rarest type of rainbow?

9 Do large or small raindrops produce brighter yellows, oranges, and reds in a rainbow?

10 Besides raindrops, what can create rainbows?

Answers: 1. raindrops
2. winter **3.** sunlight
4. René Descartes **5.** red,
orange, yellow, green, blue,
indigo, violet. **6.** behind the
person **7.** It is fainter than the
primary rainbow and the
colors are reversed. **8.** lunar
rainbow **9.** large raindrops
10. waterfalls, fountains,
hoses, and sprays of water
behind boats

Words to Know

acrylic: a type of plastic

air pollution: harmful materials, such as chemicals and gas, that make air dirty

arc: a curve or part of a circle

centuries: hundreds of years

forecast: predict

galaxies: large groups of stars

leprechaun: an elf in Irish folklore who must give his hidden treasure to whoever catches him

lunar: to do with the moon

mathematician: a person who studies mathematics

myths: legends or stories passed on for many generations

philosopher: a person who studies the meaning of life

proverb: well-known expression that states a general truth or gives advice

radar: a system that uses radio waves to locate objects in the atmosphere

Index